Dear Parent:

Congratulations! Your child is taking the first steps on an exciting journey. The destination? Independent reading!

STEP INTO READING® will help your child get there. The program offers five steps to reading success. Each step includes fun stories and colorful art. There are also Step into Reading Sticker Books, Step into Reading Math Readers, Step into Reading Write-In Readers, Step into Reading Phonics Readers, and Step into Reading Phonics First Steps! Boxed Sets—a complete literacy program with something for every child.

Learning to Read, Step by Step!

Ready to Read Preschool–Kindergarten
• big type and easy words • rhyme and rhythm • picture clues
For children who know the alphabet and are eager to begin reading.

Reading with Help Preschool–Grade 1
• basic vocabulary • short sentences • simple stories
For children who recognize familiar words and sound out new words with help.

Reading on Your Own Grades 1–3
• engaging characters • easy-to-follow plots • popular topics
For children who are ready to read on their own.

Reading Paragraphs Grades 2–3
• challenging vocabulary • short paragraphs • exciting stories
For newly independent readers who read simple sentences with confidence.

Ready for Chapters Grades 2–4
• chapters • longer paragraphs • full-color art
For children who want to take the plunge into chapter books but still like colorful pictures.

STEP INTO READING® is designed to give every child a successful reading experience. The grade levels are only guides. Children can progress through the steps at their own speed, developing confidence in their reading, no matter what their grade.

Remember, a lifetime love of reading starts with a single step!

For Ben, Aaron, Eve, Margot, and Baby-to-Be
—C.H. and E.T.

To Carolyn,
for her attention to detail and sense of humor
—D.P.

www.stepintoreading.com

Educators and librarians, for a variety of teaching tools, visit us at
www.randomhouse.com/teachers

Library of Congress Cataloging-in-Publication Data
Hapka, Cathy.
How not to start third grade / by Cathy Hapka and Ellen Titlebaum ; illustrated by Debbie Palen. — 1st ed.
 p. cm. — (Step into reading. Step 4 book)
SUMMARY: The first day of school becomes chaotic when third-grader Will's younger brother, Steve, arrives for kindergarten.
ISBN 978-0-375-83904-7 (trade) — ISBN 978-0-375-93904-4 (lib. bdg.)
[1. First day of school—Fiction. 2. Brothers—Fiction. 3. Schools—Fiction.] I. Titlebaum, Ellen. II. Palen, Debbie, ill. III. Title. IV. Series. PZ7.H1996Hos 2007 [Fic]—dc22 2005030497

Printed in the United States of America
10 9 8 7 6 5
First Edition

How Not to Start Third Grade

by Cathy Hapka and Ellen Titlebaum
illustrated by Debbie Palen

Random House New York

First-Day Jitters

Hi, my name is Will.

Today is my first day of third grade. I can't wait to see my friends and talk about soccer camp.

There's just one problem. Today is my little brother Steve's first day of school, too. He's starting kindergarten.

If you have a little brother and he's anything like Steve, you know *exactly* why I'm worried.

Mom handed us our lunches.

Mine was in a brown bag. Steve's was in a superhero lunch box.

Steve looked at my lunch, then at his. "I want a brown bag like Will!" he cried.

As usual, Steve got what he wanted.

"Time for school, Buster," Steve sang out. "Let's go!"

But Mom put a stop to that idea. She said dogs and school don't mix. Buster could ride to school with us, but he couldn't go inside. She called it a "compromise."

I wasn't sure what that meant. I guess it's another word for "Steve gets his own way."

In the car I set my lunch bag on my left knee. Steve set his lunch bag on his left knee.

Mom was going on and on about what a big deal Steve's first day of kindergarten was. But I was more concerned about *my* first day.

I whispered to Steve, "If you see me in the hall, just walk on by like you don't know me."

Steve giggled. "Who are you? I don't know you," he said. "Hey, Mom, who's that sitting next to Buster?"

Mom didn't look amused.

That's when I learned Back-to-School Lesson #1: Your mom will never see your little brother for the monster he is.

Off to a Bad Start

When we got to school, Buster rushed toward the door. But Mom called him back and shut him inside the car. Buster howled.

"I don't know why you're so upset," I told Buster. "You aren't the one who has to go to school with your little brother."

Mom took Steve's hand. "I'm not a baby," Steve complained. "I want to walk into school with Will!"

By then I was almost to the door. I pretended I didn't hear him.

"Will," Mom called loudly. "Please walk your brother to his classroom."

We walked inside. I tried to act cool and pretend Steve wasn't there.

It wasn't easy.

"Wow! This is great!" Steve shouted. "Hey, there are real lockers and everything!" He ran over and banged on the closest locker.

After that, things only got worse.
Steve raced through the halls. He jumped
up and down. He yelped like Buster does
when you accidentally step on his tail.

People were staring at Steve like he had two heads and three arms. I had to do something.

I grabbed him. "I forgot to warn you," I whispered. "Principal Smiley is an alien robot. If you make too much noise, her wiring shorts out. It's horrible!"

Steve gasped. "Really?"

Just then I spotted some of my friends walking toward us.

"Really," I said. "You'd better get to your classroom *right now* or Principal Smiley might find you!"

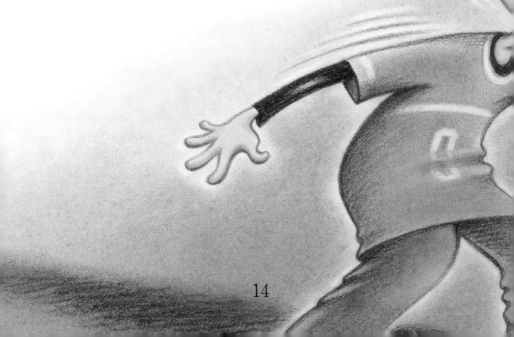

Nothing scares Steve. Or so I thought.
I mean, how was I supposed to know he
was terrified of robots?

"I won't let her catch me!" he shrieked.

He whirled around and raced down the
hall in a panic. He was heading straight
toward my friends.

Uh-oh. What had I done?

Steve and half my friends ended up on the floor.

One of them helped him up. It was Chelsea. Oh, no! She's only the best soccer player in the third grade! I wanted to crawl into a locker and hide.

Chelsea smiled at me. "Hey, Will," she said. "Isn't this your little brother?"

Back-to-School Lesson #2: Never let anyone see you in the hall with your little brother. If you do, you'll be sorry!

Just then Mrs. Kerfuffle, the kindergarten teacher, walked over to my brother.
"You must be Steve," she said. "Are you
ready to start kindergarten?"

Steve looked worried. "Can Will come,
too?" he asked.

Mrs. Kerfuffle smiled. "I'm afraid not,"
she said. "But I have some pet mice who
really want to meet you."

"Mice? Cool!" That made Steve forget
all about me *and* alien robots. He skipped
off to class without a backward glance.

Whew! Maybe now my school day
could go back to normal.

From Bad to Worse

By late morning I had almost forgotten
about Steve. I stared out the window as
Mr. Duffy droned on and on about fractions.
Outside, the playground was sunny and
peaceful and quiet.

Then, suddenly, all that changed.

And I bet you know why.

Yup. It was Steve.

I watched in horror as Steve charged through the flower beds. He was shouting and grinning from ear to ear.

And he wasn't alone. All the kindergartners were following him. They were picking flowers, jumping up and down on the swings, running around in circles, and dancing on the picnic tables. They were acting like Buster does after Steve lets him share his Mega Sugar Spots cereal.

I slid down in my chair. It was a good thing Principal Smiley wasn't really an alien robot, or we'd all be in trouble.

THWAP!

Startled, I looked up. Steve was pressing his face and greasy hands against the window. Chunks of half-chewed graham cracker sprayed out of his mouth as he laughed.

"Will! Hey, Will!" he yelled. More graham cracker gunk flew everywhere.

Chelsea was sitting in front of me. She looked at Steve, then turned around.

"Hey, Will," she said. "Isn't that your little brother?"

"Will!" Steve howled. "Come outside! This nature walk is so much fun!"

The other kindergartners came running over. They all started laughing and pounding on the window and shouting my name.

By then my whole class was looking out the window. I was the only one who wasn't laughing. Well, except for Mr. Duffy.

Back-to-School Lesson #3: When starting school with your little brother, DON'T sit near the window!

From Worse to Horrible

". . . And then the goalie tripped and I kicked the ball over her head," I said. I was telling everyone at my lunch table about the big final game at soccer camp.

"Cool." Chelsea opened her lunch bag. "So did you win the game?"

"Yeah," I said proudly. "By two goals."

I dumped my lunch onto the table. My friend Jack looked at it and laughed.

"Yo, Will," Jack said. "What's with your lunch?"

Lying on the table in front of me were a sticky sippy cup and a peanut butter and sardine sandwich—Steve's favorite.

Back-to-School Lesson #4: Always make sure you pick up YOUR OWN lunch!

My face turned bright red. I quickly shoved Steve's lunch back into the bag.

Suddenly Chelsea looked under the table. "Something just ran over my foot," she said.

Out of the corner of my eye, I saw
something white and furry flash by.

Nearby, I heard someone scream.

Uh-oh.

"Mice!" a girl shrieked.

Steve ran into the cafeteria with the other kindergartners right behind him.

I should have known.

"Have you seen our mice?" Steve cried.

That was a dumb question. The mice were everywhere. They rushed down the aisles and around the tables and chairs. They leaped into lunch bags and onto kids' laps. Mr. Duffy was standing on his chair.

"Got one!" Chelsea cried, holding up her lunch bag. Something was wriggling inside.

Food Fight!

I didn't think things could get any worse.

Then I heard a familiar bark.

I couldn't believe my eyes. Buster charged into the cafeteria, flinging slobber left and right.

"Huh?" I said. "What's *he* doing here?"

Buster isn't a very graceful dog. He ran around, chasing mice and crashing into things. Once in a while he stopped to play with a kindergartner or steal someone's food.

It dawned on me that Buster and Steve are a lot alike.

"Hey! That dog's eating my pizza!" a girl cried from somewhere behind me.

"You know what that means," someone else shouted. "FOOD FIGHT!"

I ducked as a Tater Tot whizzed past my head.

Within seconds, food was flying everywhere. A blob of gooey cheese hit me on the shoulder.

Suddenly I heard an extra-loud scream.

Buster was standing with both front paws up on Principal Smiley's dress. He barked and wagged his tail. Then he gave her a big, wet, doggy kiss.

Principal Smiley pushed Buster away. She had two big, pizza-stained paw prints on her dress.

"Hey, Will," Chelsea said. "Isn't that your dog?"

Back-to-School Lesson #5: Mom was right—dogs and school don't mix!

A First Day to Remember

It had to be a record.

It was only the first day of school, and there I was outside the principal's office with Steve and Buster. Buster was licking dried pizza off Steve's elbow.

Principal Smiley hung up the phone and came out.

"Your mom is coming to pick up Buster," she said. "She told me he got loose when she was running errands."

"He came to see *me*," Steve said proudly. "I guess he missed me a lot."

While we were waiting, the lunch period ended. The cafeteria doors opened and kids came streaming out.

Soon we were surrounded. Everyone was talking at once. And they were all talking about Steve!

"Lunch will never be the same again!" someone said.

"Steve really knows how to have fun!" someone else added.

I was amazed. Steve was a celebrity!

Chelsea pushed her way through the crowd. "Hey, Will," she said. "Your little brother is cool."

Soon the bell rang and the other kids went back to class. I sat there and wondered if Chelsea was right.

Could my twerpy little brother actually be . . . cool?

"School is fun," Steve said. "Your friends are nice, Will."

"Thanks," I said. "They think you're nice, too, I guess. I'm not sure what the teachers think, though."

I laughed as I remembered Mr. Duffy standing on his chair. And Principal Smiley's face when Buster slurped her.

"At least you keep things interesting," I told Steve.

Just then Mom walked in.

Buster started barking.

"Hush, Buster," Steve cried. "Principal Smiley's an alien robot—if you're too noisy, she'll explode!"

Back-to-School Lesson #6: Never think that starting school with your little brother could be anything but a total and complete disaster!